TOO
Small
Tola
and the Three Fine Girls

Books by the same author

Too Small Tola

Anna Hibiscus
Hooray for Anna Hibiscus!
Good Luck, Anna Hibiscus!
Have Fun, Anna Hibiscus!
Welcome Home, Anna Hibiscus!
Go Well, Anna Hibiscus!
Love from Anna Hibiscus!
You're Amazing, Anna Hibiscus!

The No. 1 Car Spotter
The No. 1 Car Spotter and the Firebird
The No. 1 Car Spotter and the Car Thieves
The No. 1 Car Spotter Goes to School
The No. 1 Car Spotter and the Broken Road
The No. 1 Car Spotter Fights the Factory

For younger readers
Anna Hibiscus' Song
Splash, Anna Hibiscus!
Double Trouble for Anna Hibiscus!
Baby Goes to Market
B Is for Baby
Catch That Chicken!
Hugo

Non-fiction
Africa, Amazing Africa: Country by Country

TOO Small Tola

and the Three Fine Girls

ATINUKE

illustrated by

ONYINYE IWU

WALKER
BOOKS

Dedicated to Solomon – never forget –
those who are small can also be MIGHTY.
A.

To my little bean, in the hope that you love these
stories and drawings as much as I do!
O.I.

This is a work of fiction. Names, characters, places and incidents are either
the product of the author's imagination or, if real, are used fictitiously.

First published 2021 by Walker Books Ltd
87 Vauxhall Walk, London SE11 5HJ

2 4 6 8 10 9 7 5 3 1

Text © 2021 Atinuke
Illustrations © 2021 Onyinye Iwu

The right of Atinuke and Onyinye Iwu to be identified as author and illustrator respectively of this work has
been asserted by them in accordance with the Copyright, Designs and Patents Act 1988

This book has been typeset in Stempel Schneidler

Printed and bound by CPI Group (UK) Ltd, Croydon CR0 4YY

British Library Cataloguing in Publication Data: a catalogue
record for this book is available from the British Library

ISBN 978-1-4063-8892-3

www.walker.co.uk

MIX
Paper
FSC FSC® C101537

CONTENTS

Moji Grandmummy Tola Dapo

Tola Saves the Day

Tola lives in a run-down block of flats in the megacity of Lagos, in the country of Nigeria. Tola's sister, Moji, is much cleverer than Tola. Tola's brother, Dapo, is much faster than Tola. And even short-short Grandmummy is taller than Tola. Which makes Tola feel so small-o!

It is a rainy Saturday. There is no school on Saturday. Tola, Moji and Dapo are all at home.

But Grandmummy is not at home. Grandmummy is out selling groundnuts by the side of the road. That is her job. And her job does not stop on Saturday. Her job stops only on Sunday, for church.

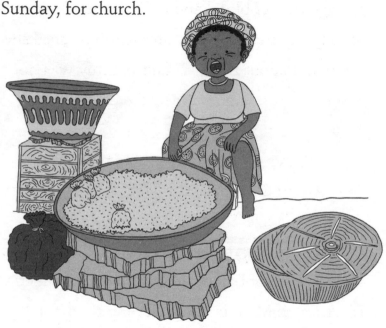

In church Grandmummy wears her most precious items – gold dangly earrings that are kept on the shelf beside her bed. Those earrings were worn by Grandmummy's own mother, and her grandmother, and her great-grandmother. When she wears them Grandmummy recites all their names, thanking them for giving her strength to carry on.

Grandmummy says that she can feel their strength in her blood and in her bones. Moji used to say that this was unscientific – until she found out about DNA. Grandmummy was not surprised. She said scientists are only catching up with what people have always known.

But church day is Sunday. And today is still Saturday. So Grandmummy is not wearing her dangly earrings. She is at work. And although Tola and Moji and Dapo are not at school, and although they do not have jobs to go to, they still have work to do.

"You three must clean the rice," Grandmummy had told them.

Tola's family can only buy cheap sacks of rice. Cheap sacks of rice have many small stones in them, stones that must be picked out.

Selling groundnuts by the side of the road does not earn them enough to buy sacks of expensive clean rice.

And Grandmummy cannot earn the money for food, and wash all of their clothes, and also clean the stones out of the rice. So Tola and Dapo and Moji have to help.

But in fact Moji is studying on the old computer that her scholarship school has lent her. She is frowning at the screen with her A* frown.

And in fact Dapo is using his knees to keep a football up in the air. He is wearing his Africa-Cup-of-Nations frown.

So in fact it is only Tola who is squatting on the floor picking stones out of the rice! From where she is she can see the bed, and the shelf with Grandmummy's gold earrings gleaming next to the Bible.

"Dapo!" she says to her brother. "You are

supposed to be helping!"

Dapo kicks the ball up with his knees faster and faster and faster. Then he suddenly traps it under his foot like a rat under a broom. He beams at Tola.

"You see that?" he asks. "You see my World-Cup moves? When I become a professional footballer I will pay for somebody to pick the stones out of the rice." Dapo paused.

"Do not worry, Too Small Tola. I will take care of you! But for now, I must practise!"

Dapo starts to kick the ball up on his knees again. And Tola rolls her eyes.

"Moji!" Tola says to her sister. "Come and do the rice with me!"

Moji raises her eyebrows at Tola.

"If I do the rice now, then I will not be able to study. And if I do not study, then I will not become a doctor. And if I do not become a doctor, then I will be picking stones out of rice for the rest of my life."

"But, Moji—" Tola says.

"Leave me alone to become a doctor," Moji says. "Then I will buy us all expensive rice. Rice with no stones."

Moji turns back to her computer screen.

Tola scowls. She always does the Saturday jobs alone.

And picking stones out of rice takes for ever.

And it is boring-o!

But Tola continues because if Grandmummy comes home and the rice is not finished, then she will not be happy. And Grandmummy might be small but her lungs are not. And that is also why Tola never tells her that Moji and Dapo do not help with the Saturday jobs. Tola does not want to hear Grandmummy shouting, even if it is not at her.

Dapo kicks the ball up on his knees again. He makes a little grunt each time he does it.

"Dapo!" snaps Moji. "You are not allowed to do that inside! Grandmummy will be angry!"

But it is raining hard
so Dapo cannot practise
outside. It is proper
Nigerian rain. The drops are as fat and as fast
and as hard as a power shower!

"And who will tell Grandmummy?" Dapo
grunts. "You, who are supposed to be doing the
rice?"

Moji glares at Dapo. Dapo keeps his
eyes on the ball. Nothing can puncture his
concentration! He is kicking faster and faster.
And grunting faster and faster too.

"Dapo!" Moji shouts. "That ball will break something! And then what will Grandmummy do to you?"

It is Dapo's concentration that breaks! The ball rolls away and knocks into Tola's neat piles of rice and stones. They become one pile of rice and stones mixed together like before.

"Look what you did!" Tola shrieks.

"I told you!" Moji sings out.

"It was you!" Dapo shouts at her. "It was you who did it. You are a witch!"

"A witch!" Now Moji is shrieking too. "Who are you calling a witch?"

Tola sighs loudly and leaves them to argue. She is so angry she could box their heads together. But they look like they are going to do that themselves. So she leaves them to it and starts to separate the piles all over again.

Then
Moji remembers
that witch or no witch
she is supposed to be studying to become a
doctor. She flashes her palm at Dapo and turns
back to the screen with her A* frown.

Dapo flashes his palm back. Shame on you!

The ball is resting in the corner of the room.
Dapo picks it up to practise again.

Moji shouts, "Go outside!"

"You want me to drown?" Dapo shouts back.

"What if your ball hits this computer?"

"You are just jealous!" Dapo accuses her. "You
know that footballers earn more money than
doctors!"

Dapo starts kicking the ball up on his knees
again.

"Anyway," he grunts, "I am not playing, I am studying."

"Studying!" Moji snorts.

"Yes!" Dapo grunts faster. "I am studying. You think you are the only one who can study?"

Moji sucks her teeth.

"Studying is hard," she says. "You, my friend, are just playing. Playing is easy."

Dapo stops. He holds out the ball to Moji.

"If you think it is easy, then you try," he says. "You try and see if it is not hard. Harder even than your studying."

Moji rolls her eyes and turns to the computer screen. Dapo laughs. He goes back to kicking the ball up on his knees.

"You see," he grunts. "You are afraid."

Quick as a flash Moji stands up and snatches the ball out of the air. She balances it on one knee. Tola watches. She watches to see if Moji is as good at football as she is at school work.

Moji jerks her knee up in the air. Immediately the ball flies across the room. Tola freezes as she watches it sail over the bed towards Grandmummy's special shelf …

… and hit it with a thump.

Tola cries out as if she has been hit herself.

Dapo groans as if he's been landed a hard punch.

Moji is silent and still as a cockroach sprayed with Flit.

Grandmummy's Bible lands on the floor with a thud.

And the earrings fly up, up, up into the air.
Tola covers her eyes.

When she uncovers them
Moji is scrabbling on her hands
and knees on the floor. Tola holds
her breath. Moji sits up holding one earring
in her hand.

Tola starts to breathe again. And Dapo laughs
a shaky laugh. Moji sighs with relief. With
shaking hands she puts the earring back on its
shelf. Then she goes back on her
hands and knees.

Moji searches, and searches, and searches for the other earring.

She looks under the bed. It is packed with Grandmummy's boxes of old clothes and Sunday clothes and things that might one day be needed. Moji pulls the boxes out and looks in each one. But the earring is not there.

Then she empties all the buckets and bowls in the kitchen corner, just in case. Some have tomatoes in them. Some have onions. Some have tiny-tiny chilli peppers. Moji spreads them all out on the floor. But the earring is not there.

Then she looks among all her books and files and papers on the crowded table. But the earring is still not there.

For a long time nobody says anything. There are only the small sounds of Moji searching.

Then, "I cannot find it!" Moji wails at last.

Her eyes are wide. She is breathing hard.

Immediately Dapo starts to search. This is not a time for quarrelling, this is not a time for blaming, this is not a time for rivalry – this is a family crisis.

Dapo looks under the chairs, and in the sack of rice.

"It must be here!" he mutters frantically.

But it is not.

He unrolls the mat he sleeps on and shakes it out.

"It must be here!" he mutters determinedly.

But it is not.

He moves Moji's piles of books and papers.

And Moji does not even complain.

"It must be here!" he mutters angrily.

But it is not.

At last Dapo wails, "Grandmummy will kill us. She will kill us."

"We must look more! We must look more!" Moji says frantically.

"Where?" Dapo asks, sitting back on his heels. "We have looked everywhere."

"We must look everywhere again!" Moji says. "Tola! Search the rice!"

Even though she knows it is not there Tola does not argue. Slowly and carefully she searches through her piles of rice. How happy she would be if the earring was hiding safe among the grains. But it is not.

Dapo and Moji and Tola search and search until all hope is gone.

Tola looks out of the window. It is still daytime. Grandmummy will stay on her spot on the Ikorodu Road selling groundnuts until night.

"There is still time," says Tola. "Still a long time to look."

So hopelessly Moji searches again under the bed. And hopelessly Dapo searches again on the table. And hopelessly Tola searches once more in her piles of rice and stones. But the earring is not there.

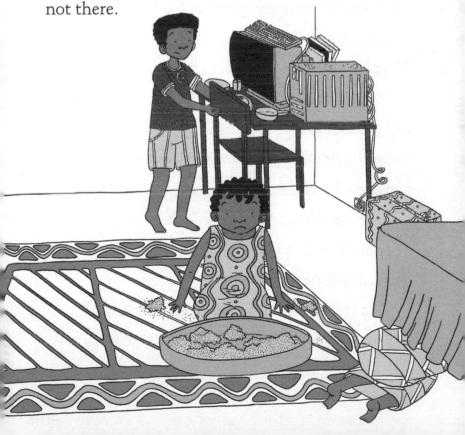

Moji lies on the floor looking at the ceiling.

"My school says that there are scholarships for doctors in Australia," she says.

Dapo sits hugging his knees.

"My coach says that China is looking for African players," he says.

Tola says nothing. She knows that Grandmummy might be short. But she can shout loudly enough to reach Australia or China when she is angry.

Then Moji says, "We had better do the rice. If we do the rice, then maybe Grandmummy will not be so angry."

Tola thinks that sometimes Moji is not as clever as she thinks she is.

"Maybe if we do the whole sack, then Grandmummy will not even notice that the earring is gone," Dapo says.

Tola thinks that Dapo is not clever at all.

Moji and Dapo jump up. Moji lights a

kerosene lamp. They squat by the sack and start to pick stones out of the rice so fast their hands are flashing.

Tola is lying under the bed where she has squeezed between the boxes to search for the earring. She is the only one small enough to fit there. She starts to wriggle out. And then she sees something glint. She squints her eyes. It glints again. In the tiny-tiny space between the heavy bed leg and the wall is something shiny.

Tola squeezes her little-little arm up between the boxes, towards the bed leg. Then she slips a tiny-tiny finger into the tiny-tiny space between the leg and the wall.

And her finger touches something smooth!

Tola hooks her finger around the smooth something and closes her hand around it. She draws her hand carefully back towards herself. Then Tola carefully opens her hand and looks. And there, resting on her palm, right in front of her eyes, is the gold earring.

Tola jumps up to shriek and bangs her head under the bed before her mouth can even open. Tola holds on to her head. She waits for the pain to stop.

And while she waits, her eyes fall on Moji and Dapo picking through the rice.

Those two never help her to do any Saturday job. Now look at them-o! Their hands are moving faster than a woman braiding hair!

Tola watches them. It is a pleasant sight to see them work hard. And as the earring is in her hand, all her worries are over. It is so pleasant that Tola continues to watch without saying anything.

And while she watches, Dapo and Moji frantically separate the stones from the rice. They forget to eat. They forget to drink. They work until the sun has reached the tops of the city's skyscrapers. They work until the sun has gone below the city's slums. They work so long that eventually Tola falls asleep.

In fact Tola wakes up only when she hears Grandmummy's heavy footsteps in the corridor outside the flat. Tola wriggles out.

On the floor in front of her is a pile of stones. And all the rice is back in the sack.

Moji and Dapo have done it all! They have cleaned the entire sack-o!

Tola hears Grandmummy's hand on the door. Moji and Dapo are cowering behind the table. Behind them Tola quickly slips the earring back onto the shelf beside the other one.

The door opens. Grandmummy enters the room with her pans and brazier on her head.

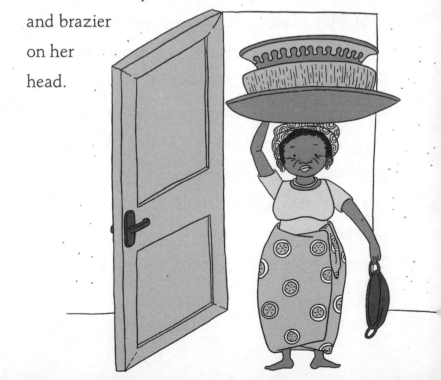

She looks at Tola and Moji and Dapo and the pile of stones.

"Good evening, Grandmummy," Tola says.

"Good evening," says Grandmummy. "You have cleaned all the rice! Well done-o! Well done!"

Then her eyes narrow slightly.

"Moji?" she asks. "You are not studying?"

"No, Grandmummy," Moji says slowly.

"Are you sick?" Grandmummy asks.

"Maybe…" Moji says.

"Hmm," says Grandmummy suspiciously.

"Dapo?" she asks. "No football?"

"It is raining, Grandmummy," Dapo says.

"Raining?" Grandmummy looks out of the window at the clear sky.

"This morning," Dapo says. "It was raining this morning."

"Hmm," Grandmummy says again, even more suspiciously.

Then Grandmummy brings out three fresh doughnuts from her basket. She holds them out to Tola and Moji and Dapo.

"Take!" she says. "You must be hungry!"

Tola stretches her hand out and takes one doughnut. Sugar sparkles on it!

"Thank you, Grandmummy!" she cries happily.

Moji and Dapo stare at her. How can she be so happy when the world is about to end?

"Moji, Dapo, *nko*?" Grandmummy asks, surprised.

Moji and Dapo shake their heads. How can they eat doughnuts when the sky is about to fall down?

"I am not hungry Grandmummy," Moji says.

"I– I cannot eat," says Dapo.

"You must be sick." Grandmummy frowns.

"I think so," says Moji.

Maybe Grandmummy will not be so angry if they are sick.

"Then you must have medicine!" Grandmummy says.

Moji's and Dapo's faces screw up. Grand-mummy's medicine is so sour it makes the insides of a person's mouth stick together.

"Take! Take!" Grandmummy gives the other two doughnuts to Tola. Then she hurries around preparing the medicine.

Moji and Dapo look at the shelf. How long will it take Grandmummy to notice that one of her precious gold earrings is gone?

But on the shelf two gold earrings glow!
Dapo's mouth drops open. Moji's mouth
drops open too. And while their mouths
are open Grandmummy pops a spoonful of
medicine inside each one.

Moji and Dapo splutter and gag. Then they
look at Tola.

Tola is looking at their doughnuts. She has already finished her own. Slowly she takes one bite out of each of her brother's and sister's doughnuts. Moji and Dapo splutter even more.

But is Tola not the one who has stopped the sky from falling down and averted the end of the world? She deserves all the doughnuts she can get-o.

Tola looks at them and then smiles her biggest and sugariest three-doughnut-eating smile!

Tola Takes Control

Tola lives in a run down block of flats in the megacity of Lagos, in the country of Nigeria. In Lagos there are people who eat pizza, people who eat pepper soup and people who eat suya and roasted corn. People who can eat morning, noon and night.

Then there are people who work every hour of the day just to put bread and sardines on the table. People like Tola's grandmummy.

While Grandmummy is working, Tola and Dapo and Moji are at school. Tola and Moji are eager to go and are never late. But Dapo is often complaining and always in trouble.

"Come on, Dapo," Moji says. "Grandmummy is suffering by the side of the road so that we can go to school."

"But I am useless at school!" Dapo whines.

When Grandmummy hears him she says, "You are useless at everything! You must try harder! Do you want to end up a street hawker like me?"

There is only one answer to that! So Dapo says nothing.

One day Tola wakes up. Something is different.

The cockerels are crowing. The room is getting light. She can hear Dapo snoring on his mat on the floor. She can hear Moji mumbling equations in her sleep. All that is normal, but still something is wrong.

Tola sits up. And there is Grandmummy, still in bed beside her!

Ah-ah! Grandmummy should have gone

to work long before dawn! She should be
squatting over her fire, ready to sell groundnuts
to people hurrying to work. Instead here is
Grandmummy. Lying in bed. Her face covered
with sweat.

Tola puts her hand on Grandmummy's arm. It
is hot like fire.

"Grandmummy!" Tola cries.

Grandmummy does not even open her eyes. But Moji wakes up.

"Wa's it?" she asks.

"Grandmummy!" Tola sobs.

Moji sits up. She takes one look at Grandmummy's hot and sweating face and says, "Call Mrs Abdul! Quickly!"

Tola jumps out of bed.

"Mrs Abdul!" she shouts as she runs down the corridor.

Tola comes back with Mrs Abdul hurrying behind her. Mrs Abdul gives a loud cry when she sees Grandmummy.

Dapo wakes up. He blinks at everyone standing around the bed.

"Mama Mighty has fever," says Mrs Abdul. "A bad fever."

Dapo jumps up.

"Grandmummy!" he cries.

Grandmummy does not answer. Mrs Abdul looks at Moji.

"Have you checked her eyes?" Mrs Abdul asks.

Moji nods. "They are OK," she whispers.

"Does she cough?" Mrs Abdul asks.

Moji shakes her head again.

"It must be malaria," Mrs Abdul says.

Moji nods her head. She is going to be a doctor so she knows.

Tola clutches her hands together. Malaria is serious! Dapo wails. He knows this too!

"Your grandmother needs medicine," Mrs Abdul says firmly. "That is all."

"We have money!" Tola says.

She runs to where Grandmummy keeps her money. She pulls out the notes from the tin. "Is it enough for one of those bottles of medicine the herbal women sell from their baskets?"

Mrs Abdul shakes her head. "Grandmummy is very sick," she says. "You will have to buy shop medicine."

Tola swallows.

"How much?" she whispers.

"Maybe five thousand naira," Mrs Abdul says quietly.

Tola gasps. She is holding only two hundred in her hand. And that is all the money they have.

Moji stands up. "We will find the money," she says to Mrs Abdul.

Tola and Dapo stare at Moji.

"I will be in my room," says Mrs Abdul going out.

Tola starts to cry. Five thousand naira! She has never before seen five thousand naira-o! What will happen to Grandmummy now?

Dapo is holding his head in his hands. Moji is wringing her hands.

"We could sell Grandmummy's earrings..." Moji whispers.

"No!" Tola cries immediately. "If we do that, Grandmummy's heart will break."

"But we have to get money." Dapo lifts his head. "Or..."

"Don't say it!" Tola closes her eyes tight. "Don't say it! And you cannot sell her earrings or all her strength will be gone."

"Then..." Moji bites her lip.

She is hopping from one leg to the other. Tola and Dapo look at her.

Suddenly Moji rushes to the wooden table. She pushes the flat table top off one of the legs. Then she puts her hand into the leg. It is hollow. And out of the hole Moji pulls a roll of money!

Tola and Dapo gasp loudly.

"Whose money is that?" Tola breathes.

"Grandmummy's," Moji whispers.

"Grandmummy's!" cries Dapo.

"But," says Moji, "she said we must never, ever spend it. Unless..." She stops.

"Unless what?" Tola asks.

"Unless Grandmummy was no longer here ..." Moji whispers.

In the bed Grandmummy moans.

"... and we were left alone," Moji continues.

Moji and Dapo and Tola stare at one another.

"If we do not spend it on medicine, then soon we will be alone," Tola says slowly.

That would be worse, she thinks ... than anything.

"We must use it to buy medicine!" Dapo says.

"So we are agreed?" Moji asks nervously.

Tola and Dapo nod vigorously.

And Moji gives the money to Tola. Tola is the best at counting.

Tola counts once. She counts twice. She counts three times.

"Along with the money in the tin, it will reach," Tola says.

"So take it-o," Moji says quickly. "Take it all and go to Mrs Abdul."

Tola takes the money, gets dressed and goes.

Mrs Abdul ties baby Jide on her back. And together they leave the flats.

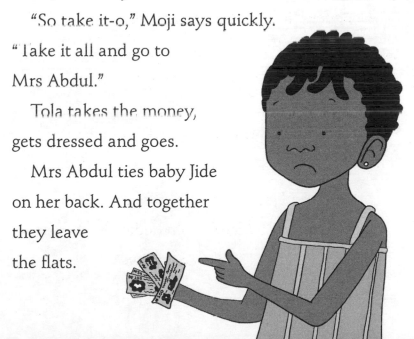

Tola feels as shaky inside as the old danfo bus that they board.

She feels as cold inside as the shop that they enter.

She feels as small inside as the look in the pharmacist's eyes as she looks down on her.

But she hands over her money and takes the medicine. And prays it will work.

"Now she will get better," Mrs Abdul says hopefully when they are back at the flats and Grandmummy has had her medicine.

"It is well," says Moji in response.

"In'shallah," Mrs Abdul replies, and leaves.

But it is not well, Tola thinks. Grandmummy is sick. And Tola is hungry. Hungry with no money and no food. They thought Grandmummy would work today and buy more.

"Moji?" Tola asks.

Moji is sitting on the bed next to Grandmummy. She is crying.

"Dapo?" Tola asks.

Dapo is lying on his mat with his face pressed down.

Tola looks at Grandmummy. If Grandmummy was well she would say, "If we are hungry and the money is gone, then we must get more!"

Then she would tie her wrapper tighter, collect her pots and pans, and set off to work.

Tola looks at her sister and brother. Moji does not stop crying. And Dapo keeps his face pressed to the floor.

Slowly-slowly Tola gets up. Slowly-slowly she reties her wrapper. Slowly-slowly she piles Grandmummy's pans on top of her head.

Moji stares at her.

"What are you doing?" She hiccups.

"I am going to sell groundnuts," Tola says.

"Are you crazy?" Dapo asks.

"No," Tola says. "I am hungry."

"But Grandmummy said that we would never become street hawkers!" Moji wails.

"Grandmummy cannot work for us now," Tola says softly. "So we must work for ourselves."

Moji cannot bear not to go to school. She looks at Grandmummy. She waits for her to say, "School is the priority. You three will never become street hawkers!"

But Grandmummy does not. She does not even open her eyes.

"O-ya!" Tola orders. "Moji, carry the sack of groundnuts! Dapo, carry the fire!"

Moji and Dapo stare at her.

Tola puts her hands on her hips.

"Maybe you two do not want to eat today?"

Slowly Moji stands up. She dries her eyes, reties her wrapper and picks up the sack of groundnuts.

Slowly Dapo gets up from the floor, rubbing his own eyes. He puts on his shorts and picks up the brazier.

Together they go to ask Mrs Abdul to watch over Grandmummy.

Tola and Moji and Dapo struggle along until they reach the place on Ikorudo Road where Grandmummy sells groundnuts.

It is a good spot near a flyover that carries many-many lanes of traffic to other parts of the city. Under the flyover a mechanic repairs cars.

Moji lights the fire and stirs the groundnuts.

Tola shouts, "Groundnut! Groooooundnut!"

Dapo is supposed to be twisting newspaper into cones but he has wandered off to watch the mechanic.

All day long Tola and Moji feed the fire and pour roasted groundnuts into newspaper twists and shout to customers. All day long they count out change and chase after cars with people holding their money out of open windows.

Night comes. The hawkers light their kerosene lamps, the traffic becomes a stream of blinding lights, and the mechanic locks up his yard and leaves.

Moji stands up with a groan. Tola counts their money. And Dapo reappears.

"We have only enough for half a loaf of bread and one tin of sardines tonight," Tola says.

Dapo wails.

"I am more hungry than that!" he says.

"We must save money to buy more groundnuts and oil for tomorrow," Tola says.

"But Grandmummy always makes more than that!" Dapo complains.

"We would have made more if you had worked too," Moji growls.

Dapo stops complaining and hangs his head.

Tola and Dapo and Moji walk home, stopping only at the night market to buy one tin of sardines and half a loaf of bread.

It is not enough to stop them from feeling very-very hungry.

Back in their room Grandmummy is still sweating. She is moaning. Her eyes are still closed.

"She will improve," Mrs Abdul says gently. "She will improve."

But by morning she has not improved. So instead of packing up their pencils and books the children go out to work in the hot sun.

Moji's throat is sore from breathing in the fumes from the fire.

Tola's throat is sore from calling after customers.

Dapo's throat is not sore at all. He has gone to watch the cars being repaired and no amount of shouting brings him back.

Day after day it is the same. Grandmummy is sick. And they have to work, not go to school.

Then one night they get back to their room and Tola hears voices. One of them is Grandmummy's!

"Grandmummy!" Tola shouts and rushes in.

Grandmummy is lying on the bed talking to Mrs Abdul. She looks weak but she smiles. And then she frowns.

"What is this?" She waves her hand weakly at the loads on their heads.

Tola and Dapo and Moji look at one another.

Grandmummy narrows her eyes. "Were you selling groundnuts?" she hisses.

"We were hungry!" Tola whispers.

"School, *nko*?" Grandmummy asks.

Moji and Dapo and Tola look at their feet.

Grandmummy frowns even harder.

"We needed money," Moji whispers.

"Moji, you knew there was money," Grandmummy says.

Moji opens her mouth. Then she closes it again.

"Moji," Grandmummy suddenly looks worried. "Moji, what of my money?"

"We bought medicine," Moji whispers.

"For you!" Dapo says hopefully.

"Medicine!" Grandmummy is horrified. "Medicine! How much did you spend?"

They all look back down at their feet. Tola can hear her heart pounding like feet running away.

"How much?" Grandmummy whispers. "How much did you spend?"

Tola and Moji and Dapo cannot speak. Their mouths have dried up like ponds before the rainy season. Their tongues, like dead fish, refuse to move.

"How much?" Grandmummy whispers again.

"All," says Moji crying.

Grandmummy slumps back in the bed.

"I am bankrupt! Bankrupt! These good-fornothing children have bankrupt me-o! And for what? For unnecessary medicine!"

"Nonsense," Mrs Abdul says loudly. "You would have died without that medicine."

"Died!" Grandmummy protests. "Who are you calling dead? I lay down yesterday and I will get up tomorrow."

Mrs Abdul sucks her teeth.

"Mama Mighty, you have been lying there for almost two weeks!" she snaps.

"Two weeks!" Grandmummy sits up again looking horrified. "Two weeks!"

She looks at Tola and Moji and Dapo again.

"You have been managing alone for two weeks," she whispers.

Then she holds her arms out to them.

"Come here," she says.

Tola and Dapo and Moji drop their pots and pans and brazier and sacks and rush forward into Grandmummy's arms.

Next morning Grandmummy is still too weak to get out of bed. But she takes charge.

"This morning," she says, "Moji must go to school!"

Moji claps her hands happily. She has missed her lessons. She has missed the quiet. She has missed her friends. And she has missed the air conditioning!

"Tola and Dapo, you must go to work now before you miss the morning customers," Grandmummy continues.

Tola stares at Grandmummy. Grandmummy looks at her sadly. Tola loves school too. Grandmummy knows that!

"But what of me?" Tola whispers.

"Your school is not like Moji's," Grandmummy says sadly. "It does not guarantee you a job. And if Moji loses her scholarship at her fine-fine school, then we will always be struggling to eat."

"Sorry, Tola," Moji whispers.

Tola turns away. She loads the pans on her

head without a word. Dapo does not complain. But he does not help either. When they get to their place on the Ikorodu Road he wanders off to the mechanic's.

"Dapo!" Tola shouts as she counts out change for a customer.

The groundnuts need turning but Dapo has his head in the bonnet of a car.

"Dapo!" Tola wails as she frantically pours nuts into newspaper.

The fire needs fanning but Dapo is underneath a car.

"Dapo!" Tola screams as someone waves for groundnuts from the window of their car.

The groundnuts are burning but Dapo is learning how to weld bits of cars onto other cars.

At the end of the day Tola marches over to the flyover. The mechanics are lounging on the cars. And there is Dapo, smiling and joking with them!

Tola marches right up behind him.

"You call yourself my brother?" she shouts.

Dapo jumps. He jumps high enough to touch the ears of a giraffe.

"What brother would let his small sister work alone while he plays around with these useless machines!"

Tola waves her hands at the cars. Dapo looks as if he wants a boot to open and swallow him up.

"She is small..." one of the mechanics mutters.

"But she is mighty," whispers another.

"Like the grandmother," hisses the boss.

Tola puffs herself up like an angry lizard ready to continue her tirade. But a shiny black

SUV pulls up under the flyover. A window opens and a woman leans out.

"I need somebody to fix my car!" she shouts.

The mechanics are still frozen by Tola's shouting. It is Dapo who defrosts first. He runs towards the SUV.

"Madam, madam, how can we help you?" he calls.

"My car is not working." The woman is panicking.

"What is wrong with the car?"

It is the boss speaking to the woman now. She explains fast.

"It sounds like the clutch," the boss says. "You need a new one."

"Please," the woman begs. "Install a new one now so that I can get my children home."

"Sorry, madam—" the boss says.

"I will pay double if you can do it now," the woman interrupts.

The boss's eyes widen, and for a moment he looks like a small child alone with a big cake. He has to screw his eyes up tightly to speak.

"I am sorry, madam," he says again.

Dapo tugs the boss's arm. He whispers in his ear. The boss's face changes. He smiles broadly.

"Madam," he says. "Of course. Do not worry. You have come to the right place. Soon your car will be purring like a leopard."

"Boss," one of the other mechanics whispers. "We have no—"

"This boy can make one fit," the boss interrupts.

Tola sucks her teeth. She waits and waits. Then she sighs and squats down to wait. She waits a long time.

By the time Dapo is finished, rush hour is over, the traffic is moving quickly, and the SUV works just fine!

A fat roll of money passes from the hands of the grateful woman into the boss's shirt.

"Thank you! Thank you!" she shouts. "I will come back. And I will send all my friends here!"

The mechanics throw Dapo up into the air and cheer. Then the boss whispers in his ear.

"Dapo!" Tola shouts. She has had enough!

"He is coming! He is coming-o!" The boss pats Dapo's back.

Tola loads the pans back onto her head. She leaves the brazier for Dapo.

"Grandmummy is going to kill you for making us so late."

Dapo says nothing. He is smiling. All the way

home he smiles. Tola sucks her teeth.

"Wait until Grandmummy gets hold of you," she says.

Dapo still says nothing. Not until he steps through their door.

"Nobody in this family," he says then, "is going to sell groundnuts any more."

Grandmummy's mouth was open, ready to shout, but now she frowns instead. Moji looks up from her books.

"What did you say?" Grandmummy growls.

"Nobody in this family," Dapo says again, "is going to sell groundnuts any more."

"Have you gone crazy?" Grandmummy frowns.

Dapo takes the money out of his vest and gives it to Grandmummy.

"This is my today's wages!" he says.

Grandmummy's eyes open wide. Tola gasps. Moji splutters.

"Selling groundnuts?" Grandmummy chokes. "You earned all of this selling groundnuts?"

"Noooo." Dapo laughs. "I am useless at selling groundnuts. I earned it fixing cars!"

"Cars!" Grandmummy splutters.

"Yes," Dapo announces. "I have a job. I am going to work every Monday to Saturday. And I will be paid this amount every single day!"

Grandmummy stares at the money. It is more than she earns in a good week!

Grandmummy looks at Dapo. She shakes her head. She blinks hard. She clears her throat.

"I have been wrong about you," she croaks. "You are not useless, Dapo."

Dapo grins.

"No, Grandmummy," he says. "You were right. I am useless at school. I am useless at housework. I am useless at selling groundnuts. But when it comes to cars – then I am mighty too!"

Grandmummy laughs. And Moji laughs.

And Tola laughs too.

Dapo looks at Tola.

"Tola," he says, "tomorrow you can go back to school."

Tola looks at Grandmummy. Grandmummy smiles and nods her head.

Tola jumps up and down and claps her hands and dances around the room. The pots and pans fall off her head and everybody laughs.

Tola laughs again too. Grandmummy is better, Dapo has a job, and tomorrow – tomorrow – tomorrow she is going back to school!

Tola and the Three Fine Girls

Tola lives in a run-down block of flats in the megacity of Lagos, in the country of Nigeria. In the city of Lagos there are girls who have their own beds, girls who have their own bathrooms, girls who have their own cars and their own drivers to drive them. Then there are girls who do not. And Tola is one of those.

Tola is on her way home from market with Grandmummy. They have bought sweetcorn, they have bought goat meat, they have bought all kinds of fine-fine food because now Dapo has a job and they can afford to eat well-well.

Tola is excited because today is masquerade day in Lagos. Tall figures with scary masks will dance in the city streets. They will twirl and whirl slowly to drums. And people will crowd to see them!

"Grandmummy, can I go?" Tola pleads as they walk home from the market. "Please, I beg you!"

Grandmummy sucks her teeth.

"Who will you go with?" she asks.

Tola looks at Grandmummy. Grandmummy raises her eyebrows.

"You see my feet?"

Tola looks down at Grandmummy's feet. They are so swollen they are bulging out of her flip-flops. Grandmummy's feet need to rest!

"How about Moji?" asks Tola hopefully.

Grandmummy snorts. "You have the power to drag your sister from her homework?" she asks.

Tola purses her lips.

"Dapo!" Tola exclaims.

Grandmummy shakes her head, exasperated.

"Your brother works hard, and by the time he gets home he is only fit to eat and sleep."

Tola nods sadly. It was true. Sometimes Dapo was so tired he fell asleep while eating.

"Maybe I could go by myself?" Tola says quickly.

Grandmummy says nothing. And nothing means *No*. Tola sighs loudly. Grandmummy ignores her. They cross the road to where the fancy shops are.

"Mama Mighty!" somebody calls out to Grandmummy.

Grandmummy stops. The man calling her is the uncle of her cousin's cousin. Grandmummy smiles. She will enjoy catching up on all the family news.

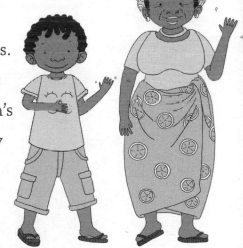

Tola stands on one foot. And then on the other foot. She does not enjoy standing outside fancy shops. She has never been inside any of those shops. They are too expensive and too cold. And everybody around is too-too fine. They make Tola feel she is not so good. But Grandmummy and the uncle talk and talk. So Tola looks into one of the shop windows.

She stares at the trainers. Sharp blue trainers, smart black trainers, cute pink trainers, sporty yellow trainers, cool red trainers…

Tola looks down at her own dusty worn-out flip-flops. She would like to wear a pair of new trainers! But when she looks at the price tags she gasps. Those trainers cost more than five times Grandmummy's malaria medicine!

Tola turns away from the window. A girl is walking towards her. A girl wearing a pink skirt and a T-shirt embroidered with a silver heart. A woman wearing big sunglasses and carrying a handbag is walking next to the girl. Neither of them notice Tola. She is too shabby to be noticeable.

"Mama?" the girl says to the woman.

Her mother does not answer. She is too busy talking into her phone.

"Mama?" the girl asks again.

"What is it?" her mother snaps at her impatiently.

The girl points to the trainers in the shop window. And without saying one word her mother pulls money out of her handbag and hands it to her daughter.

While the girl is in the shop the woman continues talking. "We will come to the masquerade," she says, "but not until later on. I have a lot to do today."

The girl comes out wearing cute pink trainers that match her skirt and T-shirt.

"Look, Mama!" she says.

Her mother looks but she continues to talk on her phone. The girl bites her lip.

Tola thinks it is a shame that the woman did not notice how fine her daughter looked. And she thinks it is a shame to look so sad when one looks so fine.

Tola looks at Grandmummy. Grandmummy is telling a long story about the business partner that her cousin had in Ibadan years ago.

Tola knows better than to interrupt Grandmummy. In Nigeria children are taught never to interrupt.

So instead she looks into the window of a shop selling blue jeans. There are dark jeans the colour of indigo and light jeans the colour of harmattan skies. There are even jeans that sparkle with diamonds!

Tola looks down at her own jeans. They are too short and too loose and the stains make them look dirty.

A girl Tola's age comes out of the shop. She is
wearing a pair of jeans as faded as Tola's. But
her jeans fit her all the way up and all

the way down. And
they have no stains
at all.

Tola stares at the
girl. Her jeans are
cool. Her denim
jacket is cool.
Her hair that
falls down her
back like a black
waterfall looks freshly done
and cool, cool cool! And her hands clutch
shopping bags with cool logos like Adidas
and Apple.

A car horn beeps loudly and a BMW with
blacked-out windows pulls up.

"Daddy!" the girl cries and rushes to the car.

A uniformed man puts his head out of the driver's window.

"Your father sent me to collect you," the man says.

The girl stops in her tracks.

"Is he at home?" she asks hopefully.

"He is busy in the office," the man says. "He will not be home until late."

The girl slumps into the back of the car with her shopping bags. Her eyes and mouth point downwards. Tola thinks it is a shame to look so disappointed when one has so many cool things. Tola sighs.

Grandmummy looks at Tola.

"O-ya," Grandmummy says, "let's go!"

Tola does not hear her. She is staring at a girl wearing a traditional buba and blouse in matching bright-red cloth with white aeroplanes printed on it. The girl's hair is styled traditionally too.

It is wound round and round
with black thread and bent
into curved shapes all over
her head.

Tola touches her rough hair in
its thick plaits. She sighs again.

Grandmummy comes to stand
right in front of Tola.

"What is the matter with you?"
she asks.

"Nothing, Grandmummy," Tola lies.

"Nothing?" Grandmummy asks. "Is that why
you are sighing every two minutes?"

"I just wish…" Tola stops.

She knows Grandmummy will not
understand.

"Wish for what?" Grandmummy asks. "Wish
for what?"

"I wish I was as fine as all these girls," Tola
says at last.

"Fine?" Grandmummy asks. "Why do you need to be fine? Do you not have a roof over your head?"

"Yes, Grandmummy," Tola says slowly.

"And do you not have more than enough food to eat?"

"Yes, Grandmummy," Tola says more slowly.

"And are you not able to go to school?"

"Yes, Grandmummy," Tola says even more slowly.

"So why do you need to be fine?" Grandmummy asks impatiently.

"Because..." Tola says, "because..." But what Tola feels does not match any of the words she knows.

"Exactly! Because nothing!" says Grandmummy. "Let's go."

Tola follows Grandmummy. She tries not to cry. Grandmummy looks at her out of the corner of her eye. Tola does not notice.

As soon as they get home Grandmummy says to Moji, "O-ya! Time to start cooking."

Moji looks up from her homework. She frowns one of her A* scholarship frowns.

"Who do you think you are looking at like that?" Grandmummy asks crossly.

Moji lowers her eyes.

"Maybe you have forgotten how to cook?" Grandmummy asks.

"No, Grandmummy," Moji says, but her eyes are back on her computer screen.

"So what are you waiting for?" Grandmummy bellows.

Moji jumps up. She rushes to gather onions and tomatoes. Tola helps. There are onions to chop and tomatoes to grind and fish to fry.

"Tola," Grandmummy says, "leave that. Loose your hair and go and wash it."

Tola and Moji stare at Grandmummy. It is not hair-washing day! Saturday is hair-washing day.

"Can you not hear me?" Grandmummy frowns.

"Sorry, Grandmummy!" Tola says.

Quickly Tola starts to loosen her hair. And quickly Moji goes back to chopping onions. Nobody wants Grandmummy to bellow again.

Tola's hair is divided into four neat sections and plaited into four thick plaits. It is all that anyone has time or money for.

Quickly Tola loosens the four thick plaits. Then she hurries down the outside corridor to the bathroom with a bucket, a jug, a towel and a bar of soap.

In the bathroom there are two taps. One should be hot and one should be cold. They are both cold.

Tola fills up the bucket with cold water. She bends over forwards and carefully pours jugfuls of water over her head. When it is completely wet she soaps her hair thoroughly. When she has finished soaping she uses the rest of the water in the bucket to rinse her hair. Then she hurries back with the towel wrapped around her head.

Back in their room Grandmummy is looking tired. She has kicked off her tight shoes and is stretching her swollen feet. But she has a comb and a jar of Vaseline on her wide lap.

"O-ya, sit," Grandmummy says to Tola, gesturing to the floor in front of her.

Tola hesitates. On Saturday Moji always plaits Tola's hair into four thick plaits. Why is Grandmummy going to do it today?

"What is wrong with you children?" Grandmummy asks again crossly. "Do I have to say everything twice?"

Tola quickly sits on the floor in between Grandmummy's knees. She decides not to risk asking any questions.

Grandmummy takes the comb. She combs out Tola's hair. It is so thick and so curly that it takes some time.

Grandmummy parts Tola's hair in half and ties one half out of the way. And then she parts the remainder in half and ties the other half out of the way. Tola waits for her to plait the remaining quarter into a big thick plait. But she does not.

No, now Grandmummy divides a tiny section off from the remaining quarter neatly with the comb. She ties the big section out of the way. And then she starts to weave the remaining section into a tiny, tiny, tiny plait.

Tola's eyes open wide, wide, wide!

Once upon a time Grandmummy used to weave plaits tinier and neater and finer than anybody else in the flats. That was before her hands became thick and old and tired from cooking groundnuts for a living.

Moji is staring at the teeny tiny plaits that Grandmummy is weaving on Tola's head.

"Do you think we will eat today?" Grandmummy asks her. "Or will you still be standing there until midnight?"

Moji drags her eyes away from Tola's head and goes back to chopping onions and grinding tomatoes.

For three whole hours Grandmummy plaits teeny tiny strands of Tola's hair together. For three whole hours she bends Tola's aching neck backwards and forwards and side to side. Tola's scalp stings as Grandmummy pulls fingerfuls of hair into plaits. But Tola does not complain. Oh no! She is having her hair weaved for the first time in her life – she has nothing whatsoever to complain about!

"Grandmummy?" Tola dares to ask after some time has passed.

Grandmummy grunts in answer.

"Did you use to weave Mama's hair?"

For one second Grandmummy's fingers stop. And so do Moji's. Then Grandmummy starts to weave again.

"I plaited your mother's hair every week when she was your age," Grandmummy says.

And then Grandmummy tells them stories of how their mother used to demand a different hairstyle every week.

"She loved to follow the fashion." Grandmummy sighs.

"Was she fine?" Tola asks.

"Of course!" Grandmummy says. "She was the most beautiful girl in the whole of Lagos."

Tola and Moji both sigh as Grandmummy weaves both plaits and stories of their mother. She makes a criss-cross pattern all over Tola's head.

Suddenly Grandmummy stops.

"Get my box from under the bed," she says. "The 'Dove' one."

Tola gets up on aching legs. Grandmummy rifles inside the box. She brings out a plastic bag. Inside the bag are beads. Shiny glittering beads.

Tola's eyes shine as brightly as the beads!

And one by one by one Grandmummy plaits the beads into her hair. Tola can feel each plait becoming heavier under the weight of each bead. She cannot believe how lucky she is!

At last Grandmummy smears cool Vaseline in between each plait and Tola's tight and aching scalp is soothed. Then Grandmummy pats her head.

"Finish," she says.

Tola scrambles up and runs to the broken mirror propped against the wall. She gasps!

Her whole head is covered with tiny interweaving plaits and near the end of each plait a glittering bead sparkles. Tola moves and her whole head shimmers.

Moji claps her hands. "Tola, you are so fine!" she exclaims.

Tola cannot stop looking in the mirror. And she cannot stop smiling. She does look so fine. She has never looked so fine in her life before!

Behind her in the mirror Tola can see Grandmummy sitting with her swollen feet resting on the floor and her swollen hands resting in her lap. Even her tired eyes look swollen.

Suddenly Tola turns around. She goes to Grandmummy and kneels down. This is the polite way in Nigeria.

"Thank you, Grandmummy," Tola says with all her heart.

She does not know if she is saying thank you for the plaits or stories or thank you, Grandmummy, for plaiting her hair even when it pains her hands. Maybe love and stories and plaits are the same thing anyway.

Grandmummy smiles at Tola with shining eyes.

"You look as fine as your mother," she says.

And Tola's eyes shine too!

"I have to go and get more gari," Moji interrupts.

"Tola can go to ask Mrs Abdul," Grandmummy says, patting Tola's cheek.

Tola jumps up. She can't wait to show Mrs Abdul her hair.

In the corridor Tola passes Mrs Shaky-Shaky.

"Beautiful!" Mrs Shaky-Shaky puts a shaky hand to Tola's hair.

"Thank you!" Tola smiles shyly.

The sound of voices makes Mama Business open her door. She stares at Tola's hair.

"Mama Mighty is plaiting again?" she asks.

Before even waiting for Tola to answer, Mama Business is knocking on doors.

"Mama Mighty is plaiting again!" she announces at each one.

She even manages to get to Mrs Abdul's door before Tola does.

"Come and look!" she shouts.

Mrs Abdul puts out her head. When she sees Tola she claps her hands too.

"Tola!" she says. "Fine-fine girl!"

Tola beams.

Mr Abdul the tailor pokes his head out too.

"Tola!" he exclaims when he sees her. "You will be the finest girl at the masquerade!"

Tola's smile shrinks small.

"I am not going," she says.

"Why?" Mr Abdul cries. "You cannot miss it!"

"Grandmummy's feet are too swollen. Moji is studying. And Dapo is working," Tola says. "I have nobody to take me." She shrugs. "It is OK. I will go next year."

Mr Abdul looks at Mrs Abdul. Mrs Abdul smiles and nods. And she nods again when Tola asks for gari.

Mr Abdul walks with Tola back to her room.

"*Salam alekum*," Mr Abdul says as he enters.

"Peace be with you too, Mr Abdul," Grandmummy replies. "How is your family today?"

"We are all well, *hamdulillah*," Mr Abdul says. "How are you and the children today?"

"We too are well, praise God!" Grandmummy replies.

"Today is the masquerade…" Mr Abdul begins.

"I know, I know." Grandmummy sighs.

"I love the masquerade," Mr Abdul continues, "but Mrs Abdul does not want to take baby Jide out into the crowds."

"She is very wise," Grandmummy agrees. "Crowds are not good for babies."

"So I must go alone," Mr Abdul says mournfully. "And it is not so good to go to the masquerade alone. It is better to go with a friend. So that you and your friend can discuss everything that you see together."

Grandmummy grunts.

"I understand," Tola says. "If I was going to the masquerade I would want to go with a friend too."

Mr Abdul smiles at her. Then he looks at Grandmummy. "If Tola comes with me I would not have to go alone," he says.

Tola opens her eyes wide and holds her breath.

Grandmummy snorts. Then she smiles.

"Off you go," she says. "Mr Abdul will look after you."

Tola jumps up and down. The shining beads bounce and sparkle! Mr Abdul laughs.

"O-ya!" he says. "Let's go! Let us not miss anything!"

Tola and Mr Abdul hurry out of the flats.

Mr Abdul gets on his big black bicycle. That bicycle is an old friend of Tola's.

Once she rode around the whole city on the back of it, taking measurements for Mr Abdul, who makes clothes for the people of Lagos.

Tola jumps onto the luggage rack. And Mr

Abdul pedals off. Like everyone in Lagos, Tola is so strong and her balance is so good she does not even need to hold on.

They ride down busy streets and bump down alleyways and sail over flyovers until they come to Surulere, the part of the city where the masquerade is happening.

All the way there Tola can feel the shining beads on the ends of her beautiful plaits bounce up and down. It feels like the love of her grandmother. It feels like the memory of her mother. Tola could sail all the way to Surulere on her happiness.

"Can you see the masquerade dancers, Tola? Can you see them?" Mr Abdul shouts when they get there.

"No!" Tola shouts back.

The streets are crowded now. And all Tola can see are the backs of people in the crowd. But she can hear the drumming. And people shouting. The masquerade must be so close!

"Climb up!" Mr Abdul shouts. "Climb up to see!"

So Tola stands up on the back of the bike rack with one hand on Mr Abdul's shoulder. Mr Abdul pedals the bike between some cars. The cars cannot get any closer.

Suddenly Tola can see!

The dancers with their carved-wood faces move slowly to the fast-beating drums. They circle and bend and bow. And their long heavy costumes sway from side to side.

"I see dem!" Tola shouts. "I see dem!"

In the cars a group of girls hears Tola shout. One is wearing a pink outfit. One is wearing skinny jeans. And one is wearing red cloth printed with white aeroplanes.

All three girls stare at Tola standing upright on the back of a bicycle. She is laughing and pointing and her hair sparkles around her face like a star!

"I wish I was allowed to ride around the city on the back of a bicycle," says the girl in the pink trainers.

"I wish I could see the masquerade," says the girl in skinny jeans.

"I don't care about the masquerade," says the girl in the red cloth. "I just wish I was as happy as that fine-fine girl."

"Me too," says the girl in the pink trainers.

The three girls look at Tola shining and they all sigh. Tola looks like the happiest girl in the world...

And that is exactly how she feels!

Atinuke was born in Nigeria and spent her childhood in both Africa and the UK. She is the author of the bestselling Anna Hibiscus and No. 1 Car Spotter series, as well as *Africa, Amazing Africa: Country by Country*. She started her career as an oral storyteller of tales from the African continent; now she writes about contemporary life in Nigeria. Atinuke lives on a mountain overlooking the sea in West Wales. Visit her website at **atinuke-author.weebly.com**

\\|/

Onyinye Iwu is Nigerian. She was born in Italy, where she spent most of her childhood, then moved to the UK when she was a teenager.

A teacher by day and an illustrator by night, Onyinye enjoys reading books, especially ones that make her laugh. Visit her website at **www.onyinyeiwu.com**